# The Adventures of Reginald Stinkbottom

Written and Illustrated by
Sophia J. Ferguson

# For Max

First published in Great Britain 2015 by Macnaughtan Books
Text and illustration copyright © Sophia J. Ferguson 2015

ISBN-10: 1517280125
ISBN-13: 978-1517280123

Reginald Stinkbottom lived in a house

With his Grandma, three squirrels, two cats and a mouse

He loved to eat beans

Eight helpings a day

"They're my favourite" he shouted

"I don't care what you say!"

Now the problem with eating huge platefuls of beans

Is the wind they produce and you know what that means

It means that there's gas inside Reginald's tummy

And when it comes out, the smell isn't funny

In Reginald's case it's much worse than you think

For it really does make the most terrible stink

Well Reginald's Grandma got sick of the smell

It grew stronger and stronger and made her unwell

"I can't live here" she howled "with this terrible pong!"

So she packed up her suitcase and flew to Hong Kong

Reginald cried for six days in a row

"Oh Grandma" he sobbed "Where on earth did you go?"

He knew he should stop eating beans but he couldn't

He thought about stopping but knew that he wouldn't

"I love them so much and the smell here is fine"

Now instead of eight helpings he's gone up to nine!

Well the stink in the house became more and more terrible

The animals living there found it unbearable

Three squirrels, two cats, not forgetting the mouse

Who usually loved being in Reginald's house

They packed up their bags. They could take it no more

Not a single goodbye. They just slammed the front door

"The smell is too much!" they complained as they went

"We're off to the country to live in a tent!"

Poor Reginald now was completely alone

He was desperately lonely with no one at home

"Does the wind from my bottom smell really that bad?

How could they leave me and make me so sad?

I bet they won't bother to write me a letter

I'll have some more beans, that should make me feel better"

So he slurped down a dollop in the usual way

And soon he was scoffing twelve helpings a day!

So Reginald's life wasn't going too well

Even neighbours were leaving because of the smell

But then something happened right out of the blue

A major event. It was something quite new

It all started one day as he walked to the shop

When his bottom let out an incredible pop!

The force of the blast blew him up in the sky

He came down with a thud and he started to cry

In somebody's garden he'd had a crash landing

And when he turned round, a sweet lady was standing

She was dressed in high heels and a pink woolly sweater

And instantly Reg knew that things would get better

"My surname is Windy-Pants, how do you do?

My first name is Gertrude, that's Gerty to you

You seem to have had a most terrible fright

You must come inside. Are you feeling alright?"

"Do come into my house and make yourself comfortable"

When she opened the door, Reg saw something incredible

All over her house he saw tins of baked beans

Reg thought to himself "She's the girl of my dreams!"

Well Gerty loved beans. She was simply unstoppable

And the wind from her bottom was frankly phenomenal

So Reggie and Gerty grew terribly fond

It seems that they shared an extraordinary bond

But guess who arrived back at Reginald's house?

Yes, Grandma, the squirrels, the cats and the mouse

"I missed you" cried Grandma "I don't mind if you pong"

"I've been desperately homesick, I hated Hong Kong"

The animals too had been terribly miserable

Life in their tent had been very uncomfortable

So they all settled back into Reginald's home

But Reggie had something to tell them this time

"While you were away something happened to me

I made a new friend. She's called Gerty, you see

Gerty loves beans. She breaks wind just like me

We have so much in common, I think you'll agree"

"Gerty and I, we share the same vision

And we've come to a very important decision

I've decided to move into Gerty's abode

She lives round the corner, just off the main road

You can visit on Tuesdays and Fridays for dinner

I think you'll agree this solution's a winner"

Well Grandma appeared to be rather relieved

The animals too were secretly pleased

So Grandma, the squirrels, the cats and the mouse

They get to live in a sweet smelling house

But they love going to dinner at Reggie and Gerty's

On Tuesday and Friday for beans at six thirty

And Reginald now has the happiest life

It's all thanks to Gerty. She'll soon be his wife

The best part of all is that she thinks it's funny

When Reginald squeezes the wind from his tummy!

If you enjoyed this book, you may also enjoy:

"Grandpa Mudcake and The Crazy Haircut"
by Sophia J. Ferguson

Check out Reginald Stinkbottom's website:
www.reginald-stinkbottom.com

Printed in Great Britain
by Amazon